THE OLDEST STINGER IN TOWN

BURCHETT & VOGLER

Illustrated by
Tim Archbold

BLOOMSBURY
CHILDREN'S
BOOKS

For Zöe May, with love

First published in Great Britain in 1999
Bloomsbury Publishing Plc, 38 Soho Square, London, W1V 5DF

A CIP catalogue record of this book is available from the
British Library

ISBN 0 7475 4270 8

Printed in England by Clays Ltd, St Ives plc

10 9 8 7 6 5 4 3 2 1

THE OLDEST STINGER IN TOWN

Old Buttspry Primary School

OB
PS

Name: Mabel Agnes Gladstone Muttley

Class: 5

Teacher: Mr Dibble

English	Written - Mabel would make better progress if she could be persuaded to use pen and paper instead of her slate. Spoken - Mabel is never at a loss for words. Unfortunately.
Maths	Mabel usually finishes the Numeracy Hour in ten minutes and spends the rest of the time polishing her abacus and tidying out her handbag.
History	Mabel has a vast knowledge of twentieth century history, but must get out of the habit of writing as if she was there at the time.
Drama	Mabel enjoys these sessions and makes imaginative use of her handbag.
Music	Since Mabel's first class singing lesson, when we all spent half an hour looking for a wounded cat, Mabel has been put in charge of the maracas.
Design Technology	All Mabel's work has been made with items she keeps in her handbag. Her scale model of Buckingham Palace made using hair curlers, corn plasters and an old corset has been much admired.
PE	Mabel is very sprightly and shows a lot of enthusiasm. However, she would do better if she put down her handbag.
General comments	Mabel has settled in quickly to Old Buttspry Primary and is a very popular member of the school. She obviously feels at home, as she wears her bedroom slippers in the classroom. Although Mabel shows a degree of independence well beyond her years, I am concerned about her need to cling to her handbag.
Head Teacher's comments	Well done, Mabel. Targets for next term - try not to take over Mr Dibble's history lessons. Remember that staff cannot be expected to come round at playtime with tea and biscuits. Try not to refer to members of staff as 'young so and so'.

Head of School .... *Bleat.* ....

Class Teacher .... *Mabel* ....

Days late   0

Days absent   0

One

It was nearly nine o'clock and pupils were spilling in through the gates of Old Buttspry Primary School.

Mabel Muttley, dressed in her baggy school uniform, pedalled cheerfully along on an ancient tricycle. Her glasses bounced up and down on the end of her pointed nose and her beads rattled as she went. Jodie Bunn clung on the back with her eyes shut as the tricycle creaked and clattered over the pavement.

'Can't I get off and walk, Mabel?' yelled Jodie. 'I want to get to school in one piece!'

'Don't you worry, dearie,' Mabel called over her shoulder to her friend. 'My

Bortwhistle Boneshaker has never let me down yet!'

The tricycle screeched round a litter bin, wobbling on two wheels.

'Aren't you a bit old for a trike?' asked Jodie. She leaned forwards and whispered in Mabel's ear. 'After all, you are a hundred and nine.'

'A hundred and ten in August!' said Mabel proudly.

'Not so loud, Mabel!' hissed Jodie in alarm. 'Someone might hear!'

Mabel Muttley was a rather unusual junior school pupil. No one, apart from Jodie, knew she was a century older than the rest of the children in class five. A hundred years ago, Mabel had left Old Buttspry Primary to work as a servant but she'd always promised herself that one day she would come back and finish her education. And here she was. The teachers thought she was rather wrinkly for a nine-year-old, but they'd seen her birth certificate and it seemed to be all right. They hadn't noticed that Mabel had accidentally held her thumb over the year of her birth.

'Let's have some music,' cackled Mabel. 'I'll get me wireless out.'

She took her hands off the handlebars, and, still pedalling, rummaged in her handbag and produced an old radio. She hooked it over the front of the trike, plugged it into a dynamo under her saddle and twiddled the dials. Music crackled out. Mabel whistled tunelessly along as she turned into the school gates.

'Splutter, whiz, hiss . . . Coming up to nine o'clock!' announced the wireless, 'and it's a Radio Buttspry special newsflash! Calling all youngsters. The Old Buttspry Playhouse is starting rehearsals for a new production . . .'

'Sounds interesting!' said Mabel. She started pedalling vigorously in circles round the car park, getting in the way of a large black chauffeur-driven limousine that was trying to pull up.

'Stop!' yelled Jodie. 'I'm falling off!'

'Sorry, dearie!' chortled Mabel. 'I have to keep the wheels turning or the radio won't work! Try and hang on.'

She turned up the volume.

'. . . THE THEATRE IS LOOKING FOR

ENTHUSIASTIC CHILDREN TO
AUDITION FOR THIS NEW MUSICAL!'
blared out the wireless. 'ANYONE
INTERESTED SHOULD COME ALONG
TO THE PLAYHOUSE TONIGHT AT SIX-
THIRTY . . . CRACKLE, SPLUTTER . . .'

Mabel squeezed hard on the brakes and
Jodie fell off.

'Did you hear that?' Mabel exclaimed as she pulled her friend to her feet and brushed her down.

'I expect they heard it on the other side of town!' muttered Jodie, rubbing her bruises.

'Let's go along tonight and audition!' Mabel went on chirpily. 'I haven't trodden the boards since I was at the London Palladium.'

'But aren't you forgetting one thing, Mabel?' said Jodie. 'They only want children.'

'Nonsense, dearie,' said Mabel firmly. She chained her trike to the railings. 'You're as young as you feel, as Grandma Muttley said when she entered the under-fives' sack race on her eighty-seventh birthday.'

There was an angry hoot and the

limousine finally managed to park. The
back window glided down.

'What do you think you're doing,'
growled a voice, 'messing about in my
parking space? I'm going straight to the
head teacher. You're in big trouble!'

Two

An angry-looking man in a smart suit got out of the back of the limousine.

Mabel marched flat-footedly up to him.

'Councillor Scrimshanks!' she exclaimed, shaking him eagerly by the hand. 'Good to see you, sir! Me and Jodie were just listening to the wireless. Miss Bleat always says we should keep up with the news – and we wouldn't want to disobey the head teacher, would we, sir?'

Cedric Scrimshanks looked at Mabel as if she might bite. As local councillor and school governor, he considered himself to be in charge around Old Buttspry Primary. Everyone was scared of him. Miss Bleat even gave him her special cushion in the staffroom. However, since Mabel had arrived, things had changed a bit.

'Don't let it happen again,' he grunted. 'You've made my Sidney late.'

'I am sorry!' cackled Mabel. She and Jodie turned to go into school. 'We know how much Sidney loves working,' she called over her shoulder.

'Shirking, more like,' muttered Jodie.

When they'd gone, Sidney Scrimshanks, nastiest boy in class five, slunk out of the car. He was carrying a school bag and a pot marked 'Supa-slime – stains greener than green'.

'Did you hear that on the radio, Dad?' he whined.

'Couldn't help it, son. Don't worry, I'll tell Miss Bleat she's not to allow loud noises on school premises.'

'I'm not talking about the noise,' snapped Sidney. 'I meant the play. I want to be in it.'

'Then I'll take you to the auditions myself,' said his father.

'But Dad,' whinged Sidney, 'that stupid Mabel Muttley will tell everybody about the play and all the class will be there and they'll be having fun and I hate it when they have fun and they'll get all the parts and . . .'

'Don't you worry, my boy. I'll speak to the director. You shall be the star!'

By the end of the day, news of the auditions had spread. Class five were meant to be spending the last lesson doing weights and measures, but most of them were busy preparing for their evening at the Playhouse.

With one hand, Mabel weighed some
fossils on an ancient pair of kitchen scales
she had produced from her handbag. With
the other she had an imaginary sword
fight. Jodie was doing a tap dance and
measuring the length of the floor at the
same time. Mr Dibble, their teacher, came
over.

'At least you two are getting on with

your work,' he said wearily. 'But, Mabel, how many times do I have to tell you to use grammes instead of old-fashioned pounds and ounces?'

'Those newfangled weights are too fiddly, sir,' said Mabel firmly. 'I'd lose them in me handbag.'

Sidney Scrimshanks watched the class practising for the auditions. They were wasting their time. Once his dad had spoken to the director at the theatre, they wouldn't look so cheerful. He couldn't wait to see their faces when his name was in lights above the Old Buttspry Playhouse.

Jodie came to the end of her dance with a clatter and bent down to read her tape measure. Sidney's weaselly face screwed up into an evil grin. He crept up behind her with a handful of Supa-slime.

Before he knew what was happening he found himself tangled in the tape measure, with Mabel's wrinkly face peering at him.

'Sorry, Sidney,' she cackled. 'Didn't see you there. I was giving Jodie a hand with her measuring.'

'Just you wait, Mabel Muttley!' snarled Sidney, struggling to free himself. 'I'll get you for that.'

'You'd better wash the slime off first,' suggested Mabel. 'It stains something shocking!'

'Thanks, Mabel,' said Jodie as Sidney hopped off, still trussed up. 'He's such an odious weasel.'

'Them Scrimshankses are all the same,' declared Mabel. 'I remember when I was at school with Sidney's great-great-grandfather. He tried to set light to the school inspector. It was lucky I accidentally threw a bucket of water over them.'

The bell rang.

'Want a ride home, Jodie?' asked Mabel.

'No thanks,' said Jodie. 'I intend to be in one piece for my audition tonight.'

Three

That evening, the Old Buttspry Playhouse was full of children. They wriggled in their seats, chattering with excitement, as they waited for their auditions.

'I hope I get picked! I've been practising all day.'

'Bet Mabel gets a part.'

'Yeah, do you remember when she did her 'Charge of the Light Brigade' with rollerblades and a hatpin?'

'Mr Dibble was gobsmacked!'

'Glad Sidney's not here to spoil everything.'

A worried-looking man stepped on to the stage and frantically waved a clipboard.

'Silence please!' he called. 'I am Quentin, the director. Now, you will all know the sad story of the Pied Piper who rids Hamelin Town of a plague of rats. He lures them to their watery deaths with a tune on his pipe but the Mayor refuses to pay him the money he's been promised. The Piper takes a dreadful revenge. He entices the children away with his pipe and they are never seen again.'

The director paused and fixed the children with a dramatic stare.

'I, Quentin Tarantello Smith, have turned this classic tale into 'RATS – the Musical', a tragic masterpiece that will have the audience weeping into their hankies. A show that the whole country will be talking about. A massive production with hordes of youngsters and a scurrying army of rodents. However, we're on a tight budget and there aren't many costumes, so I'll need nine children and six rats. And I only want kids who can sing in tune.'

'That's me,' cackled Mabel.

Jodie groaned. Mabel had been banned from singing after her first lesson at Old Buttspry Primary when class five had started searching for a wounded cat, and the rest of the school had left the building, thinking the fire alarm had gone off.

The auditions started. The children trooped up on to the stage one by one to sing a song to the director. Soon he had a list of names on his clipboard, including Jodie's.

'I'm going to be a rat!' Jodie gasped to Mabel. 'I can't wait.'

'Anyone left?' called the director, peering into the auditorium. 'We're running out of time.'

'Just me, sir!' called Mabel, waving her handbag and marching flat-footedly up the aisle. 'I'm going to do 'Knees up, Mother Brown'.'

As soon as she reached the spotlight, she hoisted up her skirt and began leaping around the stage, screeching out her song as she went.

yaaaooo!!

Quentin the director stood astounded, Jodie slid down in her seat and the other children put their fingers in their ears. A stagehand rushed on with a first aid kit.

'Call an ambulance!' he yelled over his shoulder. 'Someone's had an accident!'

Quentin staggered over to Mabel and held up a trembling hand. 'I've heard enough,' he croaked. He turned to the waiting children. 'Now, all those who've got a part, come up to the stage to try on costumes. The rest can go.' He looked at Mabel. 'And that includes you.'

'But I haven't finished, sir,' declared Mabel, pulling a telescope out of her handbag and closing one eye. 'I haven't done me 'Death of Nelson' yet.'

'You'll be the death of me if you carry on,' said Quentin weakly.

'I'm not budging until I have a part in your play, sir,' said Mabel stoutly. 'It won't be complete without me, as Grandma Muttley said when she joined the sponsored human jigsaw.'

'But look here,' said Quentin in desperation. 'There aren't any more rat outfits and anyway, I can't have that racket in my musical . . .' He looked at Mabel, with her determined expression and her flat feet planted firmly on the wooden boards. He walked over to the side of the stage and called into the wings. 'Gloria, love, we haven't got any other costumes, have we?'

'Just this one,' came a voice, 'left over from when we did 'A Sting in the Tale'.'

An enormous black and yellow striped ball came zooming through the air and landed on the stage with a thud.

Quentin sighed with relief and shrugged his shoulders.

'That's it then, I'm afraid. There are no bees in my play.'

But Mabel was already struggling into the huge, furry, moth-eaten costume.

'It fits me perfectly, sir,' she chortled, standing there with the spare legs dangling and the antennae twitching. 'I'll be off now to practise me buzzing.'

'I give up!' exclaimed Quentin. 'Just stay

at the back where you can't be seen, get rid of the handbag and remember – bees don't sing!'

'Thank you, sir!' said Mabel, shaking him firmly by the hand with one of her six legs. 'You won't regret it.'

Jodie ran up to her, dressed as a rat. 'This is brilliant, Mabel!' she exclaimed. 'I'm

glad you're in the play as well. And best of all, Sidney's not around to put a spanner in the works.'

'Not so sure about that, dearie,' said Mabel, scratching her arms. 'Me elbows are itching!'

Mabel's elbows always itched when there was trouble about – and that usually meant the Scrimshankses.

'Your elbows have got it wrong this time,' declared Jodie. 'Sidney's not here.'

At that moment, the doors at the back of the auditorium burst open. Sidney swaggered in with Councillor Scrimshanks and Chubby Charlie his driver.

'Wonderful!' called the director. 'Just what I need.'

Four

'Should have known Sidney would turn up in the end,' whispered Jodie crossly.

Councillor Scrimshanks's driver settled down in the front row of the stalls with a large bag of popcorn. Sidney and his dad climbed on to the stage. Sidney strutted up and down and bowed to an imaginary audience.

'I knew you'd want my son to be the star of the show,' said his dad pompously to the director.

'I'm not talking about the star of the show!' squealed Quentin. 'But look at his face. I've never seen a more rat-like boy. He's perfect.'

Sidney stopped mid-bow and tugged his father's sleeve.

'But I want a big part,' he whined.

'That's right,' said Councillor Scrimshanks. 'If my boy's going to be a rat, he'll be King Rat.'

'Hear, hear!' called Chubby Charlie.

'You took the words out of my mouth,' exclaimed the director. 'Gloria, love,' he called, 'get out the garden twine. We need another set of whiskers . . .' Then he turned pale. 'But I forgot, we haven't any more costumes!'

'I'll provide Sidney's outfit,' said Councillor Scrimshanks importantly. 'Nothing but the best for my boy.'

Sidney smirked at the thought of the smartest costume in the production. A giant bee walked up and shook his hand.

'Congratulations, Sidney,' it cackled. 'You'll be a perfect rat!'

Sidney scowled at the bee. He was horrified to see Mabel's face grinning out at him. He wasn't going to share the limelight with her.

At that moment he noticed a rope with a hook on the end, hanging down at the side of the stage. He looked at the hook, then he looked at the back of Mabel's costume, where a large loop stuck out between her bee's wings. Sidney crept off sniggering.

The director clapped his hands.

'Attention everyone,' he called. 'I want to see all children and rats in their costumes now. Remember, Bee, keep out of sight and definitely no singing!'

The young actors milled about the stage, adjusting their outfits. Mabel skipped nimbly off, wings flapping behind her and handbag firmly over one of her bee's knees.

The rats lined up and started to learn a few dance steps, accompanied by a piano in the orchestra pit. Mabel had just taken a duster out of her handbag to give her sting a polish when all of a sudden she found

herself hoisted high into the air. She could
see Sidney lurking in the scenery below,
pulling on a rope.

'Bless my bloomers!' she cackled as she
dangled over the stage. 'I'm flying! Well, I
might as well make the most of it, as
Grandma Muttley said when she found
herself locked in the cake shop and ate all
the doughnuts.'

Mabel waggled her legs and flapped her wings in time to the music as she swung cheerfully across the stage above everyone else's heads. She could hear Sidney snickering below.

'This'll get you chucked out of the play,' he sneered.

Quentin the director was rooted to the spot. Finally he found his voice.

Marvellous, luvvy

'That was marvellous, luvvy,' he called up to Mabel, as Chubby Charlie clapped enthusiastically. 'I've never seen such a natural on the wire. Where's my pen? I must change the musical immediately. The bee is going to be an important character who will fool the piper and save the children – but the handbag has to go.'

Sidney stamped his foot in rage and let go of the rope. Mabel plummeted towards the stage and landed on top of him.

'Thanks for breaking me fall, Sidney,' she said brightly, picking herself up and waddling off to the wings.

'Dad!' whined Sidney, limping over to his father. 'That stupid Mabel Muttley jumped on me and she's going to be a star and it's not fair. I don't want to be King Rat any more, I want to be the bee.'

'If you want to be the bee, son,' said Councillor Scrimshanks, with a nasty laugh, 'you'll be the bee. We'll just have to get Mabel Muttley to buzz off.'

Five

The next day Councillor Scrimshanks had a bee costume made for Sidney. And not just any old bee costume. It was specially designed to fit only Sidney's weaselly shape. At the touch of a button the wings flapped realistically, the antennae flashed and the sting glowed bright yellow. Sidney couldn't wait to get rid of Mabel and take over her role as the flying bee.

Jodie and Mabel arrived early at the first rehearsal. Mabel was wearing her bee outfit.

'We're not supposed to be in costume until the dress rehearsal,' Jodie told her.

'Nonsense, dearie!' cackled her moth-eaten friend. 'I can't possibly play the part of a bee if I don't look like one.'

She plodded across the stage and peered at the trapdoor in the centre of the boards.

'This gives me an idea for me final scene,' she cackled. 'I'm going to find out how it works. Stay here a minute.'

'But Mabel, I wanted to show you my dance.'

'Won't be long!' called Mabel as she scuttled off into the wings.

Jodie sighed and plonked herself down against a painted tree. Suddenly she heard low voices from the front row.

'All you've got to do is ruin Mabel Muttley's costume, son.' It was Councillor Scrimshanks. Jodie knelt up and listened through a hole in the trunk. 'The theatre haven't any money to replace it, so you can step forward with your outfit and help them in their hour of need. And as it only fits you – you'll be the bee.'

'How can I ruin her costume, Dad?'

came Sidney's weaselly voice. 'She won't take it off. She even wore it to school today.'

'You're a Scrimshanks, my boy,' said his father, with an evil leer. 'You'll think of something. Come on, let's go and grab you the best dressing room.'

Jodie heard Sidney sniggering as he followed his father out.

Suddenly there was a clatter and the trapdoor sprang open. Mabel's head popped up, antennae bobbing.

'This will do nicely for me dramatic last scene,' she cackled as she clambered up on to the stage. 'I must see Quentin straight away.'

'Wait, Mabel!' said Jodie. 'Sidney's up to something. I heard him talking to his dad. He wants the part of the bee.'

'No Scrimshanks can come between me and stardom!' declared Mabel. 'I remember when I did me Dance of the Sugar Plum Fairy at school and Sidney's great-great-grandfather put tin tacks all over the stage. I just got into me hob-nailed boots and carried on.' She gave Jodie a cheery smile. 'Don't worry, dearie. Nothing is going to stop me being the bee.'

Six

As soon as the rest of the cast arrived, Quentin the director appeared on stage and clapped his hands impatiently.

'All rats up here please,' he called. Jodie and five other children skipped forwards enthusiastically. 'Remember,' said the director, 'you're an army of ravenous, rampaging rodents. You're going to overrun Hamelin Town. You're evil, sly and nasty. I want the audience to hate you. Now, where's your king?'

He caught sight of Sidney, clutching a large pair of scissors and tiptoeing across the back of the stage after Mabel.

'Brilliant!' he called. 'Everyone look at Sidney. I've never seen a nastier bit of sneaking in my life! Get behind him and copy his every movement.'

Sidney was furious. Wherever he went he was followed by six reluctant rats. They even traipsed after him to the toilet. How was he going to cut Mabel's costume to shreds with them on his tail?

'Keeping an eye on him, dearie?' cackled Mabel to Jodie as the line of children trailed past, trying to look as sneaky as

Sidney. 'Better to be safe than sorry, as Grandma Muttley said when she wore a suit of armour to feed the chickens. Now, where's our director? I've just had a brilliant idea for scene four.'

As the rehearsals went on, Quentin was kept busy writing extra scenes in for Mabel. The best one was at the end. Mabel, with a rousing cry of 'I've come to save the children!' would dive-bomb the Pied Piper and spear him with her sting. Then she would rescue the children and, with her dying breath, stagger to the trapdoor and disappear in a puff of smoke.

And all the time, whenever he could shake off Jodie and the trail of rats, Sidney Scrimshanks skulked about trying to ruin Mabel's costume.

By the final rehearsal, Sidney was getting desperate.

'It's not fair, Dad!' he whinged. 'That

stupid Mabel Muttley has got a bigger part
than ever and I can't do anything about it.'

'I don't know why it's taken you so long
to ruin her costume,' said Councillor
Scrimshanks.

'My first plan would have worked,'
whined Sidney, 'if you hadn't sat on the
glue instead of Mabel.'

'My best trousers ruined!' muttered his
dad. 'Still, the paint pot on the door should
have been foolproof.'

'I thought pulling her legs off as she flew over would do the trick,' grumbled Sidney. 'How was I to know she'd have knitted herself new ones by the time she landed?'

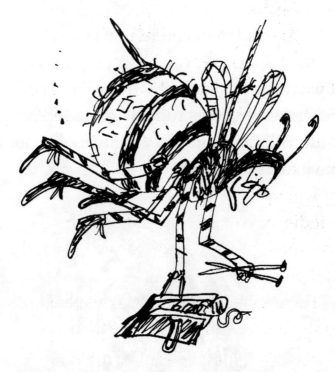

'We're running out of time, son,' said Councillor Scrimshanks grimly. 'It's the opening night tomorrow. Forget the costume. We'll have to get rid of Mabel Muttley herself! I'll tell you what to do . . .'

Seven

It was the opening night of 'RATS'. The tickets were sold out, the stage was set with the brightly painted wooden scenery of Hamelin Town and the orchestra was tuning up.

Jodie and Mabel, dressed in their costumes, peeped round the curtain at the audience.

'There's loads of people,' whispered Jodie excitedly. 'This is going to be great . . . as long as Sidney doesn't spoil it.'

'Well, he hasn't managed it yet,' said Mabel brightly. 'I'd like to meet the Scrimshanks who could spoil me big night.'

'Look!' squealed Jodie. 'There's Mr

Dibble, and Miss Bleat! And I can see my
mum! She's in the front row, next to
Councillor Scrimshanks and his driver.'

She turned to Mabel. 'It's a pity your
mother couldn't be here to see you.'

'I know, dearie,' replied Mabel sadly, 'but
she couldn't. She always goes to karaoke
on Tuesday evenings.'

*

The lights went down in the auditorium, the orchestra began to play and the curtain rose to reveal Hamelin Town overrun by six rodents.

'We're a vast army of rats!' they sang as they scurried about the stage. 'We'll nibble your coats and your hats . . .'

Chubby Charlie clapped loudly. Quentin began to search frantically in the wings.

'Where's my King Rat?' he demanded. 'He should be out there.'

In the front row of the audience, Jodie's mum leant over to Councillor Scrimshanks.

'That's my daughter,' she said proudly.

'My boy was going to be a rat,' Sidney's dad told her pompously, 'but he's got a much better part now. In fact he's the star.' There was a high-pitched buzzing noise off-stage. 'This should be him now!'

The audience gasped as a giant moth-eaten bee with a handbag flew on. Mabel's cheery face beamed down on them.

Councillor Scrimshanks jumped angrily to his feet.

'What's *she* doing there?' he demanded. 'Sidney's meant to have dealt with her. Come on, Chubby Charlie. He needs our help.'

'But I want to see what happens to the rats . . .' Chubby Charlie began.

'You know what happens to the rats!' snapped Sidney's dad as he dragged Charlie out of his seat, sending chocolates flying. 'You've watched every rehearsal!'

As soon as they got backstage, Chubby Charlie watched the play from behind a cardboard mountain while Councillor Scrimshanks stumbled about in the dark amongst a pile of scenery.

'Sidney!' he hissed. 'Where are you?'

There was a weaselly whimper from a giant papier mâché beehive and Sidney staggered out. He had a pot marked 'honey' stuck on his head.

'What's going on!' demanded Councillor
Scrimshanks. 'Why aren't you on stage?'

'It was that stupid Mabel Muttley!' came
Sidney's muffled voice. 'She did this to me.
It's not fair.'

'It wouldn't have happened if you'd
shoved her in that cupboard like I told

you!' growled Councillor Scrimshanks. He pulled the honey pot off Sidney's head. 'Go and get into your costume. Chubby Charlie, you know what to do.'

'But Boss,' protested the driver. 'I'm enjoying the show.'

'Just get on with it,' snapped Councillor Scrimshanks.

Meanwhile Mabel was buzzing busily round the stage. She flew over the heads of the townspeople, did a country dance on the roof of Hamelin's bakery, then produced a cloth from her handbag and dusted the town hall chimney. Finally she flew down and settled on a plastic mushroom while the piper promised the mayor that he would get rid of the rats.

She rummaged in her handbag and pulled out a flask, a china cup and a cake tin. She had just poured herself some tea and offered round a plate of iced fancies to the townspeople of Hamelin, when a huge net was flung over her head and she was hoicked off the stage.

'Bless my bloomers!' she exclaimed as she was carried along a corridor and thrown into a cupboard. 'I've been bee-napped!'

Eight

Jodie was getting frantic. When she and
the other rats had been lured to their
watery death by the Piper, she'd slipped
off to meet Mabel for an ice-cream. But
Mabel hadn't turned up. Jodie had hunted
everywhere. Now it was Act Two and the
Piper was leading the nine children to their
doom. In a few moments the bee should be
buzzing down from the sky to rescue them
from their fate. And Mabel was missing!
A jagged hole creaked open in the painted
hillside ready to swallow up the children.
The orchestra played a dramatic chord and
the spotlight swung to illuminate a point
high on the backdrop ready for Mabel's
entrance. Nothing happened. The

orchestra struck the chord again and the spotlight wobbled hopefully. The audience began to get restless.

'It's all going wrong!' wailed Quentin in the wings. 'First the King Rat disappears, and now I've lost my bee!'

He felt a hand on his shoulder.

'Don't despair, Quentin,' said a deep voice behind him. 'I've got a bee for you.'

'And he looks the bees knees, Boss!' added Chubby Charlie.

It's all going wrong!

'But I can't get the straps on, Dad!' wailed Sidney as he struggled with the flying harness.

'Never mind the harness, son. I'll sort it. Your public are waiting. Get out there.'

Sidney the bee leapt on to the stage and gave a deep bow. Chubby Charlie cheered loudly and Quentin collapsed with relief and fanned himself with his clipboard.

Sidney pushed a button under his arm. His wings started to flap, his antennae flashed and his sting lit up like a Belisha beacon. He strutted proudly around, buzzing.

Councillor Scrimshanks waved the harness from the wings.

'I've found out how it works, son,' he hissed. 'Quick! Put it on . . .'

But at that moment, a cry echoed around the theatre.

'I've come to save the children!'

This was the cue the stagehands were waiting for. Thinking Mabel was strapped

in her harness, they pulled on the rope to
bring her flying to the rescue of the
children of Hamelin.

To his astonishment, Councillor
Scrimshanks found himself pulled off his
feet and hoisted high above the stage. He
dangled in the air, kicking his legs
furiously, not daring to let go.

'Never seen this bit before,' came Chubby Charlie's cheerful voice.

'Bring the curtain down!' wailed Quentin. 'It's a disaster!'

At that moment the doors at the back of the theatre burst open. A round, stripy figure with a handbag rode up the dark centre aisle on a tricycle, screeched to a halt and clambered on to the stage.

Nine

There was complete confusion on the stage. The Pied Piper was wandering about in a daze, followed by nine puzzled children. An angry man in a suit was dangling on a wire and two giant bees stood eyeing each other up. The audience began to titter.

'They're not meant to be laughing!' wailed Quentin. 'This is supposed to be a tragedy!'

'Sorry I'm late,' Mabel chortled to the audience. 'I'd like to thank Sidney for standing in for me at such short notice. I got meself locked in a cupboard. Lucky there was a window in it. I climbed out on to the theatre roof, shinned down a drainpipe, somersaulted into the car park, grabbed me trike and came straight here. I'll take over now.'

'Oh no you won't, Mabel Muttley,' snarled Sidney.

'Oh yes she will!' yelled Chubby Charlie, delighted that the play seemed to be turning into a pantomime.

Sidney reached behind him, snapped off his pointed sting and stabbed viciously at Mabel.

Quick as a flash, Mabel grabbed the pipe out of the Piper's hand and fended off the blow with it. Then she flashed the pipe round her head at the speed of light, wrote her name in the air, lunged forwards and poked Sidney in the belly. Sidney staggered and fell over backwards with his legs in the air.

'Stop mucking around and get me down, boy!' shouted Councillor Scrimshanks from overhead. 'My suit's tearing.'

'That was brilliant swordplay, Mabel,' called Jodie from the wings.

'Thank you, dearie,' declared Mabel, waving her pipe at the audience. 'I used the Muttley Fencing Manoeuvre! Always came in useful when I was in the army.'

She plodded to the front of the stage and beamed at the audience.

'I will now finish with a little song. Knees up, Mother Brown.'

'No!' screamed Quentin from the wings. 'Quick, bring the curtain down!'

As Mabel opened her mouth there was a cheerful shout from Chubby Charlie.

'He's behind you!'

Mabel stopped and swung round. Sidney had finally got himself to his feet. Now he stood at the back of the stage, bristling with fury and shaking his sting at her.

'I'm going to get you once and for all!' he
shrieked.

'I'm going to get you once and for all!'
was the cue for the stagehands to open the
trapdoor for the dramatic exit of Mabel the
heroic bee. As Sidney charged furiously at
Mabel, the trapdoor opened. Sidney
disappeared in a puff of smoke.

'Ladies and Gentlemen,' announced
Mabel. 'I apologise for the interruption.
And now for my song . . .'

The curtain suddenly came down in
front of her nose with a thud.

Ten

The next morning Mabel Muttley pedalled
cheerfully to school on her tricycle, with
Jodie clinging on the back.

'You were brilliant last night, Mabel!'
shouted Jodie, as the tricycle rattled along
towards the school gates. 'I was nearly
deafened when they all stood up and
cheered. You're a star!'

'Indeed I am, dearie,' chortled Mabel. 'I
brought the house down, as Grandma
Muttley said when she got her toffee recipe
wrong and made dynamite instead.'

A large black limousine roared past

them. Sidney and his dad were sitting in the back. They glared at Mabel.

'I don't think those two will be showing their faces at the theatre again,' giggled Jodie.

'Nonsense, my girl!' declared Mabel. 'I've promised Quentin we'll do the same ending every night. Sidney's got a starring role, just like he wanted.'